THE BIRDING BODY

Written by Oliver Bestul
Illustrated by Veronica Swanson

Performed in 50 states

Orange Hat Publishing
www.orangehatpublishing.com - Waukesha, WI

For information, please contact:

Orange Hat Publishing
www.orangehatpublishing.com
Waukesha, WI

www.orangehatpublishing.com

This file contains a transcript of my tape-recorded notes on the Veery case. As usual, I have enhanced said recording with further descriptions of the evening's events where needed, as I remember them. The sketching talents for which my grade school assignments' margins were infamous among my teachers have also been employed, visually describing every important detail I saw in the kitchen of Violet Veery.

I have also, as usual, included the imagined comments of the victim, in italics, because this casefile would seem at once incomplete and confusing without them. These comments were, of course, unrecorded, but they helped me solve yet another case, and so deserve the attention I here give them. They act as a testament to the so-called overimagination for which I was chided as a youth, an overimagination that has created the detective I am.

It began on an impossibly foggy evening.
My eyes were on my feet, the only things
I could see, as I toed my way closer to the
back door of Violet Veery. I'd driven into
town the morning prior, sent to investigate
the murder of Celine Saker. On this foggy
evening, however, I'd come to file a report
on the apparent suicide of her neighbor,
the woman whose home I was just about to
enter. As I did so, I began my recording:

"I've entered the back door and am now
standing in what looks to be a kitchen," I
said. It was a plain space. The open shelves
on the wall to my left were nearly empty; I
placed the briefcase I carried on the teal-
tiled countertop beneath them. My usual
feelings of congestion in such a kitchen were
diluted, however, by a wall of glass.

"I'll be, what a window! I'm looking
at a massive picture window, only fog
to be seen outside. And what an odd fog
it is, thick. The window looks out to
my right, the victim's left. Oh, hello
miss." Studying the kitchen, I hadn't
noticed its owner. "You must be Violet
Veery. The victim faces the door and
me. Or, the culprit, I suppose. Victim
and culprit both, I suppose. She's
sitting at the far end of her kitchen
table, across from an empty seat, her
head tilted back toward the ceiling.
Detective Peterson, at your service,
miss." I took the dead woman's silence
as a sign of reticence, uncomfortable
for my speaking into a recorder. "Don't
mind the tape recorder. I take notes
this way, for later." When there came
no reply, I proceeded with my report.
"There are two bottles of wine, their
corks, a wine glass, and a pill bottle
on the table, all empty. Well, all
empty except for the corks, them being
non-containers. Just a routine report,
miss, I'll be out of your hair in a
moment." I bent to inspect the wine.
bottles, and a whistle escaped my lips.

"The wine bottles advertise two different brands, both of which I'd have to spend half a paycheck to sip, by the looks of it. The pill bottle beside them advertises a prescription for sleep medication."

DUNLIN CLINIC

DATE: THURSDAY

VIOLET VEERY

WAKE - X 10MG

DR. BROCK DUNLIN

I glanced at the shy woman. "Sleep indeed. This prescription was filled out on Thursday by Doctor Brock Dunlin. That's yesterday, the day Violet died. You certainly wasted no time in taking your medication, miss. I met with Doctor Brock yesterday, at his clinic. Poor Doc's lost two patients in a week, one just down the road from the other; Celine Saker strangled in her living room on Wednesday, Violet overmedicated here on Thursday. I guess there aren't cures for crushed windpipes or sleeping pills, anyway. He should be joining me shortly with an ambulance, Doctor Brock, to take Violet away for the autopsy." I'd forgotten where I was, as I often do while speaking. Again I noticed the deceased. "Poor thing. Attractive, young, your whole life ahead of you. Now why would you want to go and do a thing like this, miss? Come now, Violet, work with me a moment." At last, with the power of my own imagination, I convinced a reply out of the dead woman. She brought her head around to look in my direction and said

I…was…sad. Why else, Detective, over- excitement? She sounded snarky in my head. I liked her already.

"Sadness, yes, that's all it was, wasn't it. You'd just moved into town, Doctor Brock said, maybe lonesome, missing your friends." I leaned in then to read a familiar emblem on the jacket she wore.

Maybe, yes. Maybe missing my friends. Hey, buddy, what are you looking at? I can smell your breath.

"Sewn onto Violet's jacket is yet another of those patches I've been seeing so often. The Birding Body, it says."

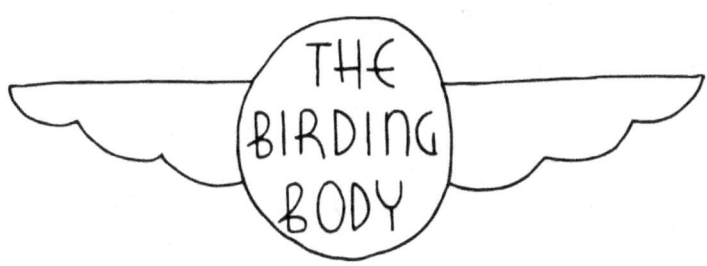

What's that, some sort of a birdbrained club?

"For birdwatching, yes." I'd had the patch explained to me a number of times since I'd arrived on Thursday morning.

Sandpiper peeping, creepy. You said you've seen the patch before?

"All around town since my arrival yesterday. Celine Saker, Wednesday's victim, belonged to the same society."

Wednesday's what? There's another stiff in town besides me?

"Celine was found in her living room on Wednesday, yes, beneath her cockatoo's cage. Her house is just down the road, in fact." I pointed in the window's direction, then at the patch on Violet's jacket. "Celine wore that same emblem, The Birding Body, along with everyone else I've met."

Ornithologists, they call them. Large eyes, sweaty hands.

"Must get some good birds in this part of the country."

Some fine feathered friends, I guess, yes. Pretty enough to paint, by the looks of it. I imagined Violet nodding her head in the countertop's direction, above which hung a string of clothes-pinned paintings.

"A row of water colors crosses over Violet's kitchen counter. Birds of the area, I suspect." I then began to take notice of the objects on the countertop.

"There's a birding book and a set of binoculars on the counter here, too. Tools of the trade, I would imagine."

If I liked cloudscapes, I had the view for it. She gazed out the window, only whiteness outside.

"The view for birding too, on any day less foggy than this."

Must have been perfect for a lonesome, young, tortured, bird-loving artist. I saw how Violet had to cock her neck to peer through the window in question.

"Then why aren't you facing it? A bird lover indeed, and the last thing you saw was the kitchen door?"

What, so maybe I liked the woodwork. What other revelations are you having, Detective? I continued my countertop inspection.

"Also on the counter sits a pull-off calendar, today's date on top. The name 'Simone' is written across it. That'll be Simone Bateleur. She was the one who found you here tonight and called it in."

Oh, I was expecting someone? I guess I wasn't much of a hostess.

"Simone, she's the older sister of Celine Saker."

Celine? Wednesday's stiff?

"Indeed. Here too sits half a dozen bottles of wine. Looks like a much cheaper brand than the ones you had last night."

Must have wanted my last few glugs to taste expensive, an aristocrat!

"Could be. Otherwise, the pricier bottles were gifted."

Must've had some ritzy friends, then! Who from, do you suspect?

"There's a card on the counter here that might answer that. It has an image of a bird on the front of it."

These people and their birds!

"On the inside it says 'Welcome to the neighborhood! We hope your move-in went smoothly today. We were so glad to hear that the house is staying in the family. Your grandfather was a good man. You must walk over soon for a visit! Until then, enjoy the gift! Your new neighbors, the Sakers.' The note's dated this past Saturday."

Saturday

Welcome to the neighborhood! We hope your move-in went smoothly today. We were so glad to hear that the house is staying in the family. Your grandfather was a good man. You must walk over soon for a visit! Until then, enjoy the gift!

Your new neighbors,
the Sakers

I moved in on Saturday? I didn't last a week!

"The Sakers, James and Celine, just days before the latter was murdered. Well, this could explain one of the wines, perhaps. Two different reds from one couple, though, that seems a stretch." Without my specific instruction, my feet began to pace.

Some of us have multiple friends, Detective. But, now, wait here a minute.

I'm an artist, a bird lover, who apparently decided to die with her eyes on a kitchen door instead of a window. To each her own, I guess. But with my nerdy birdy patch, my missed appointment with the victim's sis, and the Sakers' hello, it's starting to look like I may have had an opinion on Wednesday's murder, isn't it? And the schmoozy boozes? Something smells like fish.

"A coincidence or two too many for my taste too, I must admit."

Well, what do you make of it? I'm getting the squirms.

"I don't like to jump to conclusions, Violet, but I think you may have been..."

What? Spit it out, Inspector!

"Poisoned. They called me into town for one murder, now it looks as though I may have found a second. Wasn't quite expecting this, miss."

Neither was I, believe me. Double whammy. From my jacket, I produced a handkerchief with which to handle any other items found at the scene, happy to have only left my fingerprints on the door and the Sakers' note thus far.

"I was just stopping in on the way back to the motel from the station. Just a routine suicide, I imagined. Thought I'd assist the local law with my report, their hands and mine so full with the Saker case these last few days."

Looks as though my case might be related. A two birders, one stone situation.

"Looks to be so."

Well, do you have any suspects yet for the Wednesday woman's death?

"Celine Saker? I've got three of them."

Well done! Well detected! Who are they? Lay it on me! Opening my briefcase, I found the notes I'd typed on my first suspect and set them on the kitchen table before Violet.

James
Saker

Husband of Celine Saker
Manager at Bower Bank
Suspected adulterer
Member of The Birding Body
Had access to the house

"The first is James Saker."

The victim's old man?

"Her husband, yes. He works as a manager at the Bower Bank, the bank of choice for most of The Birding Body."

Keeper of the nest eggs, hm?

"I have here that he may have been cheating on Celine."

Dirty birdy! Who told you that?

"I jotted it down based on a comment made by Jeshan Shikra, another suspect."

Dirty birdy. Anything else on Jamesy?

"Well, he himself is a member of The Birding Body - I saw a pin on his jacket - and he of course had access to his own house."

You don't say.

"That's important. There was no sign at the scene of forced entry. My three leads are the only people besides Celine with keys to the Saker residence."

Couldn't Celine have let the killer in? People do that, you know, let people in.

"Not without an appointment."

Um, __what__?

"For the last month, Celine had absolutely every life event written down in her planner." I then produced and opened the planner in question, which I had stored in my briefcase, placing it on the table beside my notes on the first suspect. "Here, look at this. Here's this week. She had separate entries for the doctor's house calls, when her husband left for work, even the usual hour the mail was delivered."

MONDAY

8:30 AM James leaves
~10:00 AM Mail
12:10 PM Jeshan delivery
4:00 PM Simone tea
5:30 PM James home

TUESDAY

8:30 AM James leaves
~10:00 AM Mail
4:00 PM Simone tea
5:30 PM James home
6:00 PM Dr. Brock

WEDNESDAY

8:30 AM James leaves
~10:00 AM Mail
4:00 PM Simone tea
5:30 PM James home
6:00 PM Dr. Brock

THURSDAY
8:30AM James leaves
~10:00AM Mail
4:00pm Simone tea
5:30pm James home
6:00pm Dr. Brock

FRIDAY
8:30AM James leaves
~10:00AM Mail

4:00pm Simone tea
5:30pm James home
6:00pm Dr. Brock

SATURDAY

SUNDAY
Birding
Body again!

What, no entries for her bathroom breaks?
Violet began to inspect the schedule.
*Simone's all over the place; how many teas
can two sisters drink? And she saw that
doctor almost as often!*

"Yes, 'Doctor Brock' appears throughout
Celine's appointment book. She'd been sick
for weeks before she died, confined to her
home, and the doc's house calls had grown
pretty frequent. He'd usually stop in on
the way home from his clinic. He told me
Celine was just on the mend, too, that
she even had plans to bird again with The
Birding Body this weekend."

*That is a shame. Like nursing a sickly
pigeon back to health, then watching it fly
into a window pane.*

"Brock was pretty shaken over it, yes.
Over your death as well, Violet."

Over mine? Bad news travels fast!

"When Simone called in your death this
evening, Doctor Brock was the first person
I contacted. He services much of the
neighborhood – most of his patients are
birders, it seems. He should be here soon
to take you in for your autopsy."

*Lovely. But look here, Detective: Doctor
Flatline made a house call on Wednesday,
the day Celine died, right? Doesn't that
make him suspicious?*

"No. See, their appointment was in the evening, after Celine had been discovered dead. That's why we can rule him out as a suspect."

You're putting a lot of eggs in that planner basket.

"James Saker insists that his wife never met a soul without an appointment, ever since she first became sick."

Had to schedule her sneezes, I guess.

"Because Celine's time of death doesn't coincide with an appointment in her planner, James says the culprit would've had to have had access to the house."

Good ol' James told you all that, hm? He's helping out, but he's still a suspect?

"Yes, we can't let that rule him out; that might be his intention, assisting us to avoid suspicion. In fact, that brings me to my second suspect." I then produced a second set of notes, setting them atop those on the first suspect.

Simone Bateleur

Sister of Celine Saker
Unemployed
Former fiancée of James Saker
Former First Birder of The Birding Body
Had access to the house

Oh, goody! Who is it?

"Simone Bateleur, the victim's older sister. She could have called in your death today for much the same reason."

Avoiding suspicion. The sneak!

"She was also the one who found her sister dead. She called it in on Wednesday afternoon, when she arrived at the Saker house for tea, 4:03." Violet scanned Celine's planner again, finding Simone's scheduled Wednesday visit.

Looks like four o'clock is when Simone's appointment began. Is three minutes enough time to wring a little sister's neck?

"Depends on the argument. But Celine's body was already cold when the police arrived, just minutes after that. They figure she passed away around the lunch hour of that day."

So, Simone would've had to go on her little hands-on rampage before her appointment, letting herself in early.

"Her, or another one of my suspects. All three of them have the lunch hour free on workdays."

But, with Celine and then me, you're saying Simone found two stiffs in a week? This lady's either got something to hide, or plain bad timing. What else do you have on her?

"Well, Simone doesn't work, living instead off of the Bateleur inheritance, as her sister did."

I guess she _does_ have the lunch hour free. That, and every other murdering minute of the day.

"I also found out yesterday that she's the former fiancée of James Saker, Celine's widower. Simone and James lived in town together before Celine moved in and took her would-be brother-in-law for a husband."

Ouch. That must have been an awkward conversation. 'Hey, sis, nice fiancé. Remember what ma said about sharing?'

"Simone's also the former First Birder of The Birding Body. Some high distinction within the group, it would seem."

Another binocular jockey? You weren't kidding about the club's popularity.

"And as I've said, she, too, had access to the Saker home."

And I'm guessing I knew her personally, judging by the meeting we had scheduled for today, as one-way as the conversation might have been.

"It looks as though you must have known

her, yes. She called the station as soon as she found your body this evening. Good thing I happened to be there briefing the sheriff on our Saker case suspects; I heard the news of your death and volunteered to file a report on the force's behalf. It was odd, Simone said she'd come to offer you her congratulations."

For what? Turning up dead?

"She didn't say. That's all we got out of her; she was rather distraught after finding you, of course. We told her to go home and rest, and that I'd be out here right away."

Distraught, was she? What's the big deal? I'm not so scary. Got anything else on Miss Phony Simoney?

"Nothing yet."

She's all bologna, that's my bet. Now, what was the last suspect's name again? I then produced the final set of notes from my briefcase, placing them atop the rest.

Jeshan Shikra

President of The Birding Body
Supervisor at a local grocery store
Caretaker of the Sakers' bird
Had access to the house
Spoke highly of Simone Bateleur

"Jeshan Shikra, President of The Birding Body."

How did I know he'd be a member? What do you have so far for this killer?

"Jeshan works as a supervisor at a grocery store just down the road. He was also the caretaker of the Sakers' cockatoo whenever they were out of town, and for that had access to the house. You might have noticed him in Celine's planner; he'd sometimes bring the Sakers unsold produce from his store, for their bird."

Looks like the little birdfeeder stopped by during his lunch break on Monday.

"Sure, the grocery store's close enough to the Saker house for a quick trip back and forth."

Could he have come unannounced a few days after that, looking to fill his hands with neck instead of the bird's berries and carrots?

"It's possible, yes."

Very suspicious. What else do we have on him? Should we have one of our birders interview that cockatoo?

"When I asked Jeshan about Simone Bateleur, he spoke highly of her. He kept calling her a good friend, misunderstood among the members of The Birding Body."

Aren't we all? What else did he say?

"He went on to talk about the Sakers briefly. That's when he let slip something about an affair, but he clammed up when I asked for an explanation. Celine hasn't lived in town for as long as James, wouldn't know Jeshan as well, so I'd imagine it was James Saker who told him about the affair in confidence. I couldn't get anything out of Jeshan after that."

Oh great, nothing less exciting than a non-gossip.

"For the time being, I've listed James Saker as only a suspected adulterer."

And with whom, do you suppose? Don't say the bird.

"My guess? His ex, Simone, the sister. I've got a feeling their affair might've lead to Celine's death."

Sure, sure, I think I'm getting it! Celine could've found them out and approached her husband about it, yes? Maybe he surprised her for lunch that day? And he could've attacked her in the following argument! Wham, bam! That's the ticket!

"Otherwise, I suppose Simone could've killed her sister in a similar argument, having likewise been discovered as an adulterer."

And what about the caretaker, Jeshan? Could he have had his hands in this? Sweaty, little, birding hands.

"I can't quite figure how he'd be involved with the affair, nor what motive he'd have for killing Celine. He was really only listed as a suspect for having a key to the home."

Alright, the husband or the sister then. What do any of these psychopathic murderers have to do with me, Detective?

"Well, I'm guessing you knew all three personally from your involvement in The Birding Body."

Fine, but why kill me? Did I bring the bird flu when I moved in or something?

"It is a bit strange. You weren't in town a week; did you even have time to make enemies?"

Beats me. We'll need more dirt on the last few days to answer that, won't we?

"Where could I find that?"

The last few days of dirt? I don't know, a garbage can?

"Say, that's not bad! I wonder where you kept it."

Check under the sink, the cluey, cluey sink, Detective! I followed Violet's instructions, finding a garbage can in the under-sink cabinet. *And there it is!* I moved to empty the contents onto the counter, but paused for Violet's permission.

"Do you mind?"

I'm dead. I unloaded the garbage can's contents and began to organize what I discovered.

"Let's see what we have. Six more bottles of the same cheap wine as on the counter."

I took my hobby serious. For each bottle, I found an empty can of ham.

"Looks like you liked tinned meat to go with it."

Woof. Dining on a budget. From the garbage can, I then produced a letter from Bower Bank.

"I suppose so, based on your bank account's balance. Thirty-nine dollars, you were working with."

Too bad I wasn't born a Bateleur. How do you know that, anyway?

"I have a letter here from James Saker."

Jamesy, right, Celine's killer husband.

"And your banker. 'Ms. Violet Veery, Thank you for choosing Bower Bank as your financial service provider. We are happy to have you join the family. Below is a summary of your recent transfer of funds to our institution. Please review your balance and alert us of any discrepancies. Yours sincerely, James Saker, Manager, Bower Bank.' Then we have a balance here for thirty-nine ninety-three."

BOWER BANK

Ms. Violet Veery,

Thank you for choosing Bower Bank as your
financial service provider. We are happy
to have you join the family. Below is a
summary of your recent transfer of funds
to our institution. Please review your
balance and alert us of any discrepancies.

Yours sincerely,

James Saker

James Saker
Manager
Bower Bank

ACCOUNT HOLDER:	Violet Veery
ACCOUNT NUMBER:	02022017
TRANSFER DATE:	Monday
TRANSFER AMOUNT:	$39.93
TOTAL ACCOUNT BALANCE:	$39.93

*Forty bucks? How did I afford this house?
Not a cheap part of town, it doesn't seem
... Wait, is that counter cardboard? Tell
me honestly.*

"You were left the estate by your
grandfather, I imagine, the 'good man'
the Sakers' welcome note mentioned."

*Lucky break. Thanks, gramps. What are
those?* She pointed to a small collection
of pages I'd begun to gather from the can.

"These? Small squares of dated paper..."

From the pull-off calendar, I bet! She
pointed then toward the counter at the
calendar in question. *Woo! Which one of us
is the Detective?* I arranged the loose pages
in order on the kitchen table.

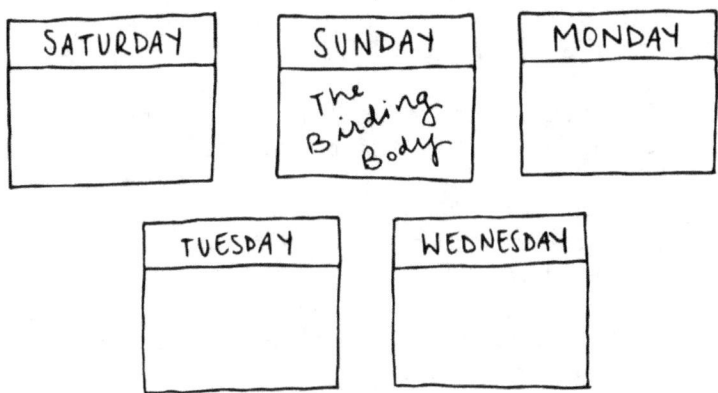

"I've got last Saturday, the day you moved in, through Wednesday. Friday's on the calendar now..."

Thursday's missing, yesterday, the day I conked. What does that one say? Violet pointed to Sunday's slip.

"On Sunday, you've written 'The Birding Body.' That must have been your first outing with the group."

The Birding Body on Sunday, Simone on Friday... If that's how I marked my deadly appointments, maybe something was written on Thursday's slip the same.

"Maybe so."

Maybe one of your suspects took it with them, didn't want the authorities to see it. Thief! Someone payed good money for that calendar, creeps! How could we tell what Thursday's said? Anything up your sleeves?

"Well, there's the pencil trick." I began to search my briefcase for the pencil we needed.

The pencil trick? The scribble test? That'll never work! Have you got one? I found it then.

"Sure do." And scratching the pencil back and forth across the top of the pull-off calendar, I began to reveal Thursday's message from the depressions it left on

Friday's slip. "It says 'Dr. Brock'.
You must have written that down as a
reminder to meet with him and pick up
your prescription." I kept scratching for
information.

Rock-a-bye pills, got it. Is that all it says?

"No, here you have 'J.S.', with a heart
beside it."

Ooh la la. J.S.? Sounds like a hunk.

"James Saker. Violet, the affair. He wasn't
cheating on Celine with her <u>sister</u>..."

He was cheating on Celine with me? Juicy!

"That gives us a new set of motives entirely. Yes, discovered by his wife, it was James who killed her in the argument. An accident perhaps, a fit of passion."

He would make sense; strangling someone does seem like a pretty personal operation.

"Then, racked by guilt, he decided to murder the woman who had brought such sudden tragedy, such complications into his life."

Little ol' me?

"You indeed."

Geeze, nice guy. And I was just starting to like this James.

"Alternatively, when Celine turned up dead, Simone instead might have decided to pay you back on her sister's behalf. She might've blamed you for the death, seeing you as James' motive. Simone might've even suspected you to be the culprit! Maybe she was right, maybe you did kill her sister!"

Take a breather, Detective! You're saying I killed Celine for a man I knew for five days or less? Some unworldly heartthrob he must've been!

"It is a bit thin."

*And what of the initials, those
incriminating little initials? It's not
Simone's on Thursday's page, but J.S.! I*
glanced again at the scribbled-on calendar.

"Right. So it was James who killed his wife."

*But he blamed me for her death? Decided to
bump me off too for it?*

"He must have."

What a loon! How did he do it?

"With your pills, I imagine. When Doctor
Brock performs your autopsy this evening,
I've got a feeling he'll find plenty of
wine and medication in your stomach."

*Right. Wait, what, James came to kill me,
but forgot a murder weapon? Not much of an
assassin.*

"True, true." I renoticed the bottles of
wine on the table then. "Maybe we were
mistaken; maybe he came here with a second
bottle of red and other intentions."

*What intentions, some sort of a sick
celebration? Goodbye, sickly wife, hello,
new kid?*

"Indeed. The wine was flowing and, in your
conversation, maybe you said this was all
too much. You found him attractive enough

to heart his initials, sure, but you barely knew the man. Maybe you intended to go to the authorities, tell them everything."

Oh, I like this version. I should've figured myself for a hero. James must have panicked, must have known he needed me out of the picture.

"Precisely, yes, but he wanted it to look like a suicide."

Sure, to prevent any of this detectivey suspicion.

"He saw the pills, here or in the bathroom, maybe, and told you, drunken, to take the rest, to get some sleep."

Poor, poor me! Poor, little, drunk me! You're onto something.

"I'm onto something indeed."

But, well, where's his glass, then? Riddle me that.

"His glass? He washed it and put it away with the rest." We both looked over at a pair of wine glasses, shelved above the kitchen counter.

There's two there, one here. Three wine glasses. That's an odd-ball number to have, Detective, even for a birder. Maybe I had four when Thursday began.

"What, you think he took his with him? Why would he do that?"

Souvenir? Evidence?

"A wine glass? What evidence is that?"

Maybe his was broken, thrown across the room in an argument, slammed down on the table in the passionate, adulterous heat of the moment! I eyed the pink tablecloth that covered the kitchen table, unblemished.

"I would think that would've left some sort of stain."

Maybe it did, Detective. Maybe the telltale stain has been staining around right under our noses!

"Excuse me, Violet." I then removed the tabletop's contents and cloth to the counter. An odd, purplish stain was revealed from underneath the pink sheet, apparently originating from Violet's direction. The stain had spattered the table's wooden surface, and had flowed around three untouched circles of varying sizes.

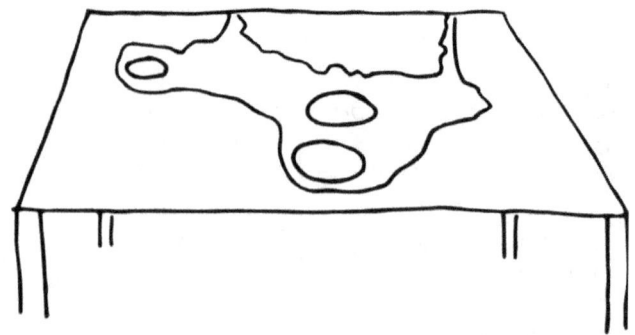

"I'll be." I grabbed again the two
expensive bottles of red. Each of them
accounted for a circle in the stain, and
were placed upon them accordingly. The
wine glass that had been before Violet
was placed upon the third, and so was now
across from her. "Here's a pair of rings
the size of those bottles, and another to
match the glass!"

Fits like a beveraged glove! Like some sort of wine cozy! But it's on the opposite side of the table.

"That's where <u>he</u> sat, in this empty seat." I pointed to the chair she was facing. "The spill came from your own glass there, Violet, tipped over sometime during the evening."

A tragic loss of wine! When, at my death?

"Perhaps. It soaked into the wood, imprinting the bottom of his glass on the unfinished surface and proving another party was present, so he covered it with a tablecloth."

Sneaky, sneaky. It looks like when my glass tipped, it rolled off the table in this direction. Violet pointed out a thinning arc of the stain that led to the table's edge. *Not bad inspecting, eh? It would have shattered at my feet!* The kitchen floor was clean.

"He must have swept up the glass and taken it with."

That conniving custodian! Wait! Maybe he missed a piece, Detective.

"Maybe he did." I checked the floor again. "I'm going to pull your chair back if you don't mind, Violet."

Go ahead, move me, Detective! And I did, uncovering a small shard of glass from behind one of the legs of Violet's chair in the process.

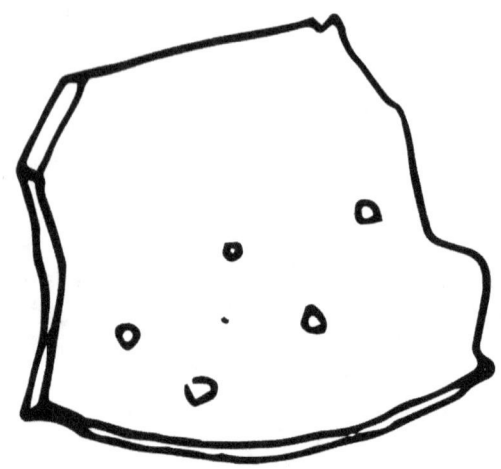

"There it is. That's a piece of wine glass alright, curved, sticky on the inside surface." I placed it on the table before Violet, and she leaned in close to inspect.

It looks like someone sneezed on it. I looked at the shard again.

"A bit of white sediment, yes. That'll be the medication. So the pills were crushed up, likely added to your glass in secret. That would explain why the pill bottle's bottom isn't included in the stain. This intact glass is missing such a sediment, of course, because it was his, and you were the only one drinking down your own medication, though you didn't know it. Violet, I think I've got it!" She sat still leaning in.

Not much of a table, this'n.

"What?" She peered up from her hunched position, her eyes wandering around.

A little shabby in this kitchen, isn't it? I hope I didn't have aspirations for interior design.

"You just moved in." I inspected the table myself. "It's a drafting table anyway, used mostly for your painting, I'm guessing, as it's facing the window." I looked again then at where Violet was sitting. "However, when you were entertaining, it seems you liked to sit on the side, so you and your guest alike could enjoy the view."

How thoughtful! Gosh, was I a good person.

"The surface cocks up this way, like an easel, and this drawer opens for supplies." The drawer was, of course, on the side where an artist would sit; I slid it open. "See?"

Look at that, those brushes are crimson, Detective! Violet pointed out a pair of the implements inside.

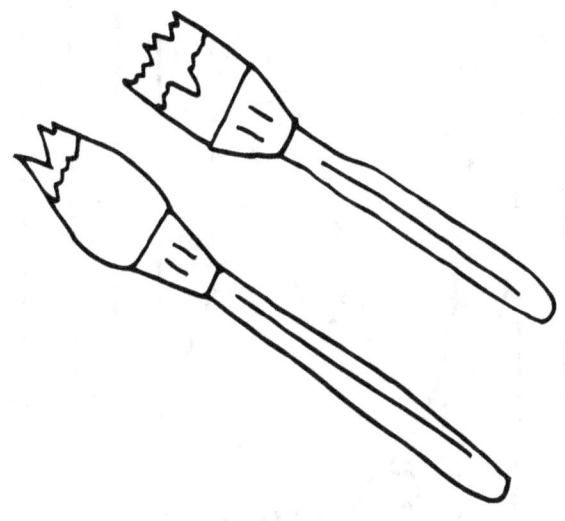

Blood! Blood, I say!

"Looks the last color you used - of <u>paint</u>, that is."

On that masterpiece there, I suppose. She nodded her head toward one of the paintings strung over her counter, that on the far right. I recognized it.

"By Jove."

What is it, not a fan of chicken?

"That's the Sakers' cockatoo, with the crimson cheek. How did I not notice?"

Oh stop, he's blushing! Odd little pet.
Wait, then I must have been in the Sakers'
home, must have taken them up on their
invitation, yes?

"That painting proves it, yes! You must've
asked to paint their exotic pet and, while
Celine was resting in bed, maybe a spark
ignited between you and her husband."

No wonder the birdie's blushing!

"You and James Saker started meeting often
after that. You had that affair, Violet, and
you're the second body to show for it!"

You got it! But, wait, Celine's creepy
planner didn't mention any painting
appointment. I went to the counter then,
to scan the planner again.

"No, no I suppose it didn't."

Crumbs. That would rule out my being
there, wouldn't it?

"It would. What did James do, bring the
bird here?"

Would've been hard to explain to Celine,
I'd think. 'Honey, I'm taking the bird for
a fly.' Something's missing here, Detective.

"Something indeed, Violet, some important bit
of evidence; I can feel it."

I can feel you feeling that bit. Well, whose purse is that? She pointed to a bag on a far end of the kitchen counter. I crossed over to it.

"Yours, I imagine."

Shall we see what bits I've got hiding in it? Maybe somebit to clear bits up a bit. I began removing the purse's contents, examining in turn each piece of evidence.

"Well, there's a receipt here from yesterday
for a pair of high-powered binoculars,
purchased on credit for – my word."

What is it? One arm, one leg?

"Three hundred dollars? For a pair of
binoculars? And here's another, again from
yesterday."

Sure, my golden binocular case!

"A field jacket. The one you're wearing, I suppose."

Needed a spot to sew my nifty patch.

"Another hundred dollars, also purchased on credit. Violet, you need to manage your money more carefully."

Too late now; can't teach a dead dog new tricks. Is that all I had?

"There's a couple crumpled ones at the bottom here, and - what's this?" I found and unfolded the purse's final bit of evidence. "A letter, miss, from another one of my suspects."

The killer! I'm sure of it! I always suspected - Who is it?

"Jeshan Shikra."

The grocery store supervisor? The Sakers'
bird keeper? What wild excitement does he
have to offer?

" 'To Miss Violet Veery, The board of The
Birding Body is happy to inform you of
your recent advancement within the ranks
of our society. Because of your astounding
skills in spotting and identification,
as evidenced by your performance in the
forest this past Sunday, you have been
promoted immediately to the position of
First Birder. I am sure your grandfather,
one of the Body's founders, would be
exceptionally proud. Your new duties can
be explained best in person. What would
you say to a cup of coffee come Thursday?
Congratulations, Jeshan Shikra, President,
The Birding Body.' " Having finished reading
the letter, I handed it to her.

To Miss Violet Veery,

The board of The Birding Body is happy
to inform you of your recent advancement
within the ranks of our society. Because
of your astounding skills in spotting
and identification, as evidenced by your
performance in the forest this past Sunday,
you have been promoted immediately to the
position of First Birder. I am sure your
grandfather, one of the Body's founders,
would be exceptionally proud.

Your new duties can be explained best in
person. What would you say to a cup of
coffee come Thursday?

Congratulations,

Jeshan Shikra

Jeshan Shikra
President
The Birding Body

Thursday? Hey, that's my deathday! I peered again at the pull-off calendar.

"I'll be. Violet, J.S. It was <u>Jeshan Shikra</u> who held your attention, not James Saker!"

And he was coming here because of my promotion? That's not very deadly.

"So it would seem. But, in that case – I'll be – in that case we've a new set of motives entirely. I believe...I believe Simone Bateleur may be behind this, Violet."

<u>I might have known</u>! Now, what makes you think so? On the counter, I found again the notes I had on Celine Saker's sister.

"I have her listed not only as the former fiancée of James Saker, but as the former First Birder."

First Birder, right. So, I took her nerdy position?

"That must have been why she came to congratulate you today, finding you dead instead."

Or so she would have us believe, eh? Maybe, though, Detective, my little friend, she came here today to make sure I was dead!

"You may have it, Violet!"

But, for being First Birder? Is that all

it was? Talk about sensitive!

"You have to understand things from Simone's perspective. She was left without a husband when her <u>sister</u> moved in, now <u>you've</u> been given her birding position, and at last she's snapped."

She wanted her life back, and she'd stop at nothing to get it! Murderous woman! Call the police! Call a detective!

"I believe your election by the board of The Birding Body may have set this whole thing into motion. Simone wanted you and her sister dead, and she got Jeshan Shikra to help her with it."

Of course! Yes! But, wait, you really think the ol' supervisor would do a thing like that?

"Indeed I do, Violet. He spoke highly of Simone, they were good friends, and so she sent Jeshan on an <u>un</u>friendly errand. He'd meet with you as The Birding Body's president, yes, but he'd come with deadly intentions."

Right, and that cute little doodle heart on the calendar means I'd taken a liking to him in the forest on Sunday, so I wouldn't have expected it!

"And as for Celine's murder, either Jeshan or Simone could have done it."

So no James Saker. I _knew_ *I liked him.*

"I suppose it wasn't James, yes."

But, wait, then what of the affair? Of the fact that I must have been in the Saker home? What do you call all that, 'unrelated circumstance'? Oh, that does sound about right.

"James must have had his affair with another party. And if you _were_ in the Saker home somehow, that event and your death are apparently unconnected. Jeshan Shikra's our J.S., Violet."

Ah, nothing like a good case-crack. She rescanned Jeshan's letter then. *Does it matter that his note mentioned coffee?*

"He must have simply brought wine instead."

The better to kill me with, eh? That'll be the other ritzy brand! She nodded toward the two expensive, empty bottles of red.

"Yes!"

But, hold your wino horses. You think Jeshan spends his supervisor's salary on expensive beverages?

"It seems so. He probably gets an employee discount at the grocery store where he works."

I wonder if they're taking applications. So he brought me a bottle of wine, apparently to celebrate my promotion, but he'd really been sent by a jealous, wicked, evil Simone with the intent to kill, is that it?

"I think so, yes!"

That henchman! We polished <u>his</u> bottle off and I opened a second, the Sakers' gift, for my final, fatal sips! But, Jeshan wouldn't have known beforehand that I was taking sleep medication, right?

"Right."

So the pills were just a convenient little discovery for him?

"Right." My enthusiasm for this hypothesis began to slacken.

Well, what was his intention before finding the pills, Detective? Drink me to death?

"Perhaps."

Perhaps <u>not</u>. Looks like I was doing that myself already. Crumbs, I thought we had it. There's a detail here we must have missed. Distracted, mishearing my companion, I peered out the window.

"There <u>is</u> no mist."

What's that, space cadet?

"The fog, it's all but cleared away since we began this investigation."

Oh, I didn't notice! Mother Nature's gas has passed. That really is a decent view I have; what a grove!

"Good for birding, I suppose."

Without all that fog, yes! My hands are sweating for some feathered action! I can see all the way to the Sakers' home from here, Detective!

"You can see all the way to... The Sakers' home, you said?" I looked from Violet to the window again.

Sure, between the trees there, isn't that it? Down the road a bit, like you said? Little cabin of death? For a better look at the home in question, I employed the pair of binoculars Violet kept in her kitchen.

"Now wait a minute, yes. Your view goes right into the Sakers' living room, where Celine was found, Violet. And there's the cockatoo you painted."

What a chicken. Maybe I never _was_ in the house, Detective. A new truth dawning, I lowered the binoculars from my eyes again.

"Maybe you never _were_ in the house indeed, Violet. You never _did_ take the Sakers up on their invitation."

I was here the whole time. Wait a minute, cue the music.

"You were here the whole time, painting the bird from your kitchen."

The last bird I painted, the blushing little chicken. What else might I have seen from this kitchen?

"What else indeed? I'll be. Violet, I think you witnessed the murder of Celine Saker."

There's my connection to all of this! A witness! How exotic!

"You saw it all unfold as you were painting the Sakers' pet!"

No wonder I needed help sleeping. Why not go to the police?

"You went to the killer instead - yes! Jeshan Shikra! You already had an appointment with him the following day, so you waited!"

For what purpose, Detective? Congratulate him on a job well choked?

"Blackmail. Extortion."

Ah, wait a minute, right! Thursday's big spending on credit, the binoculars and jacket! I expected to come into some money, didn't I, Detective? Thought I'd spied my way into a fortune; I am a creepy birder, aren't I, Detective!

"It all makes sense, yes! You thought you could get some money out of the culprit. That's it!"

Sneaky, sneaky! Jeshan strangled Celine Saker –

"On Simone's behalf, mind you."

And I saw it! Then, I demanded cash from him yesterday when he came over for a visit. Juicy!

"Panicking, he saw your sleep medication, ground it up when you weren't looking – in the bathroom, perhaps – and slipped it into your glass as the visit progressed!"

Simone came over today to make sure the poisoning was a success! Conspiracy! Poor, poor me, I'll say it again!

"That's it!"

But, hold the celebration. Again with his position, does Jeshan Shikra have the kind of money for me to want to cheat it out of him? I feel like a big-fish kind of woman.

"A grocery store supervisor? Perhaps..."

And what of the heart beside his name? The doodle on the calendar, I mean.

"You were interested, yes. Had a crush, perhaps."

And I wanted to blackmail him? Not exactly romantic.

"I suppose not, I suppose not."

What's more, if Jeshan hadn't been planning to kill me all the while, Simone wouldn't have made an appointment before I died to make sure I was dead. Do pay attention, Detective, are you following this?

"Right, yes!"

Right. So something doesn't add up again, my investigative friend.

"Crumbs. Something doesn't add up indeed, Violet."

No one else had access to the house? Not a single murderer?

"No one else." I consulted the open

planner again. "And besides Simone's afternoon tea, Doctor Brock's evening house call was the only significant Wednesday event in Celine's planner. But again, she'd been dead for hours by then."

Well, maybe Mister Honest the Doctor paid Celine a visit earlier in the day, just not on business.

"But it's like I said: every single life event was written down in Celine's appointment book, even casual visits."

Maybe Celine didn't want this kind of visit recorded. Wink wink, Detective. Hubba hubba, Detective! What was it Jeshan Shikra mentioned?

"The affair?"

The affair! Ding ding ding! The affair! Throw the confetti! Candy for the children!

"I'll be."

Maybe over the course of her long illness, Celine and Doctor Brock began a little not-so-innocent how-do-you-do relationship. He'd make his house calls in the evenings when James was home, yes, but he'd also made a practice of sneaking in a lunchtime visit!

"Sure, yes! That would explain why Celine began planning her days so vigorously after she became sick."

She couldn't have anyone walking in unexpected. 'That's not a very medical examination!'

"Right, right! But Jeshan must have done just that, stopping by the house for another one of his lunch-hour produce deliveries, only this time without an appointment. He discovered the affair on accident, bringing food for the cockatoo on a whim."

Wowie! Bet he'll never go unannounced again!

"He wouldn't give me any information on the affair, probably to keep James Saker from hearing about it, Celine already dead. Jeshan must not have realized it had anything to do with the murder."

Geeze, great job, Jeshan! Never count on a non-gossip! So, Celine and Brock got to playing doctor on his off-the-book visits. Then what, she was healing too quick?

"Precisely right, Violet! Celine was getting better, wanted things the way they were again, to bird like she used to, to have her new neighbor over for dinner. She wanted to enjoy her life again, to call the affair off, and during his final, unrecorded visit, the doctor exploded!"

Like a bomb with a doctorate! And while painting the chicken, I saw it all happen!

"Hoping to take advantage of the situation, you thought you'd invite the doctor over for an extortive conversation, even wrote it on the calendar."

Knowing he'd been seen strangling Celine Saker, Doc Brock filled me out a neat little prescription for sleep medication!

"He ground the pills up and brought them with him here, an expensive bottle of wine to boot."

The popular doctor? Sounds to me like he could afford it! We sat so we could both look out the window, at the Sakers' place, me gloating to the doc how I'd seen it all happen!

"And while you two drank through both his bottle and the Sakers', your glass was being poisoned."

When I spilled it over, he covered the stain and his scheming tracks with a tablecloth of death!

"He saw his name on the calendar, so took the page with him, along with the broken glass!"

Me and Jeshan Shikra, my little crush, must have met earlier, maybe at a café somewhere, to talk birdy over a cup of innocent joe!

"And Simone Bateleur was here today to offer her sincere congratulations, like she said, for your promotion."

Her walking in on the dead versions of her sister and me, sheer coincidence!

"Doctor Bock's our culprit!"

More confetti! More candy! Tell me you can prove it, Detective! My eyes landed then on the pill bottle now sitting on the counter.

"I sure can! Fingerprints!"

Whose? His? On what? His?

"The pill bottle, Violet!" With my handkerchief, I replaced the bottle on the table before her.

Well, sure, yes, great, of course it will have Doctor Brock's prints on it, he prescribed it, Detective!

"Of course, yes, but it will be missing another set."

Whose, the chicken's?

"Yours, miss. Doctor Brock was the only one to touch this medication, the murder weapon, I'm sure of it. You never knew the bottle existed, never held it at all; your missing prints will <u>prove</u> the doctor's guilt, Violet!"

Bless my beautiful ignorance! A sudden knock sounded from the back door then. *Eek! I've got the squirms again, who is it?*

"The doctor just arrived for his final house call, I suspect." I crossed to the door, producing a pair of handcuffs from inside my jacket.

The doctor! The villain! Look alive, Detective!

"Look dead, Violet!" And her head rolled back into place, in my imagination. "Nothing like a nice arrest to start the weekend!"

And the doctor was indeed arrested, and with the evidence against him would later plead guilty to the murders of both Celine Saker and Violet Veery. Another case was cracked, and I was on the road again.